The COVERED BRIDGE

story by Anico Surany

pictures by Leonard Everett Fisher

Holiday House · New York

For my friends in Kent

THE COVERED BRIDGE

Silver, silver, the old covered bridge creaked above the winding river.

Its worn timbers had always sighed beside the tiny town of East Greening.

Sherman and his friends, the children of East Greening, loved the rickety bridge. When they played around it, the hours quickly melted into bedtime.

Sherman and the other children, noses red and hands mittened, skated on the river in Winter. And the shivering bridge leaned against the North Wind and protected them from its frosty fingers.

When the slanting rains of Spring drummed on the
roof, Sherman fished from the bridge's windows.

Splash! The bridge turned into a diving board in
Summer. Playing pirate, the children walked its planks
and jumped into the swimming hole.

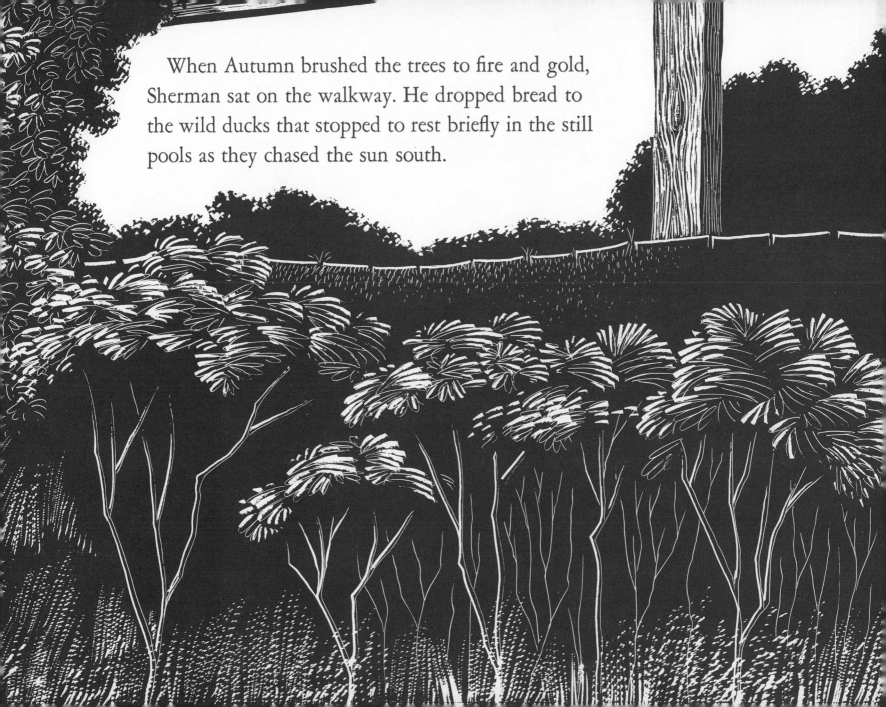

When Autumn brushed the trees to fire and gold, Sherman sat on the walkway. He dropped bread to the wild ducks that stopped to rest briefly in the still pools as they chased the sun south.

But the first selectman of East Greening hated the covered bridge. It was too old-fashioned for him. He only liked new, useful bridges.

That's all he talked about in town meetings. "Our bridge is a disgrace," he raged. "It's falling apart. Too narrow to boot, so only one car can pass at a time."

"And dirty," the first selectman roared. "A zoo lives
in those rafters under the roof. Two chipmunks, three
squirrels, six barn swallows, four bats, and one owl!"

But the first selectman of East Greening hated the
covered bridge. It was too old-fashioned for him. He
only liked new, useful bridges.

That's all he talked about in town meetings. "Our
bridge is a disgrace," he raged. "It's falling apart. Too
narrow to boot, so only one car can pass at a time."

"And dirty," the first selectman roared. "A zoo lives in those rafters under the roof. Two chipmunks, three squirrels, six barn swallows, four bats, and one owl!"

"What this town needs," he'd say, pounding his fist on the table, "is a new, practical bridge of concrete and steel."

"Mmmm, a new bridge," the people in the meeting always mumbled in reply. "We should think about getting a new bridge." And then they forgot to think about it.

But Sherman and his friends didn't care what the first selectman thought about their bridge.

They went on feeding the zoo in its rafters. They still laughed and played games in its wobbly shade.

And each time the first selectman looked at the bridge one more board had crumbled, one more ragged hole winked at him.

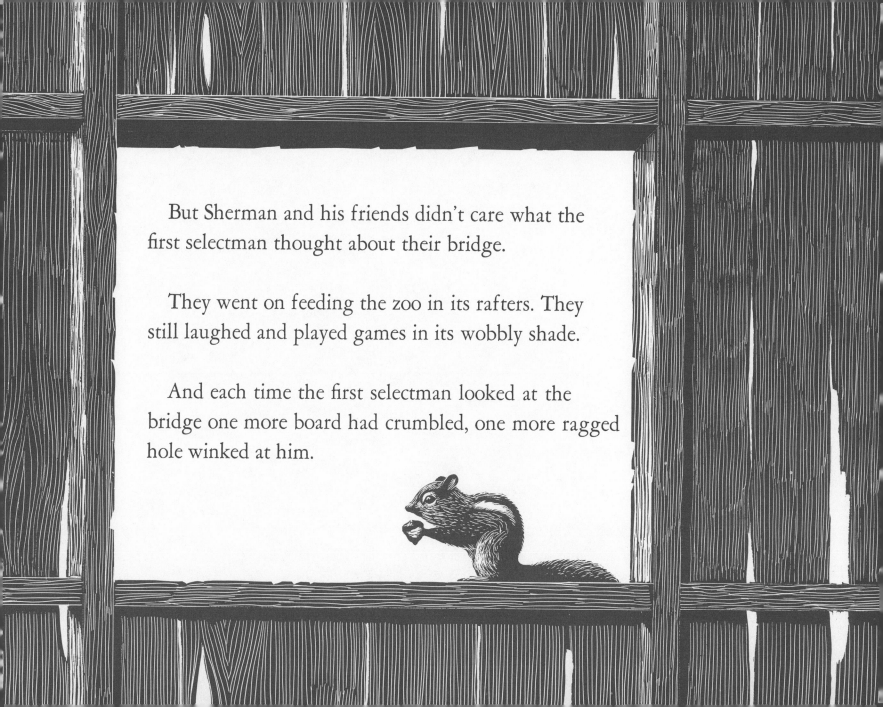

The first selectman became so angry about the
tumbled-down bridge that he called a special
town meeting.

Sherman and the children listened in secretly at the
windows of the town hall.

"We're going to get rid of that eyesore," the first
selectman shouted, "once and for all."

He talked so loud and he talked so long that, at last,
the people in the meeting agreed with him.

"Aye," everyone voted. "Down goes the old bridge.
We'll build a modern bridge of concrete and steel."

"Oh, no," Sherman whispered to his gang. "Tear down our bridge? They can't do that, a new bridge won't be any fun."

"Come on," Sherman waved to his friends, "follow me. I've got an idea."

Early the next morning, East Greening awoke to a frightful noise. BANG, BANG, BANG! It sounded like an army of hammers.

Everyone rushed out of their houses. Led by the first selectman, the people ran toward the terrible din.

They were flabbergasted at what they saw.

For the covered bridge crawled with children banging away with hammers. Egged on by Sherman, they were patching up the holes with old lumber they'd collected from every garage, tool shed, and barn in East Greening.

The bridge was plastered with wooden bandages!

"Great day in the morning," the first selectman gulped, "look at that bridge."

"Sherman, children," their parents shouted, "get right down before you fall."

"But we're fixing our bridge," Sherman yelled back, "so you won't have to tear it down."

Suddenly, their parents understood why the children were trying to save their bridge. They realized how they, too, would miss the beautiful bridge whose silver timbers had been there since forever.

They called another town meeting. This time
Sherman and his friends sat in the front rows. Led by
the first selectman, the people voted to repair the old
covered bridge and build the new bridge of concrete
and steel up the river.

The new bridge would be to drive over.

The covered bridge would be to look at and love.

ANICO SURANY and her husband live in New York City, but spend weekends at their house in Kent, Connecticut where a covered bridge like the one in this story is still in use today. The author is Hungarian by ancestry, grew up in Central America, and was graduated from the University of Southern California. Her many books include KATI AND KORMOS, THE BURNING MOUNTAIN, and RIDE THE COLD WIND.

LEONARD EVERETT FISHER has illustrated more than 100 books for children, including 13 that he has written. He has also worked in many other phases of art: as teacher, painter, lecturer, and muralist. He was born in New York City, studied art there, and holds a master's degree in fine arts from Yale. He, his wife, and their three children now live in Westport, Connecticut.